W9-BDP-635

The Family of Ree

Written and Illustrated
by Scott E. Sutton

This book is dedicated to my mother and father, Walter and Scottie Sutton, who got me started in art, and to my dear wife, Susie, who has backed me up all the way.

First Edition

A special thanks to my wife Susie, her mother Flo Conley, Tom Morgan and L. Ron Hubbard for all their help.
Inspirations for this book are from the booklet "The Way to Happiness".

Published by

SUTTON PUBLICATIONS, INC.

EDUCATION THROUGH IMAGINATION
TM

Irvine, Calif.

Printed in Hong Kong by South Sea International Press Ltd.   ISBN 0-9617199-1-5

Reading books is like digging up gold.
You get to have all the treasures they hold.

If you find a word you don't understand,
then ask your parents to give you a hand.

It may be hard and a little bit scary
but learn to look up words in a **Dictionary**.

It's a book that tells you what words mean
and it's one of the best books I've ever seen.

This book belongs to _____

The Planet of Ree

I'm going to tell you about a place
Way out there, in outer space.
A planet whose colors are blue and green,
Sort of like pictures of Earth you've seen.

The planet's name is the Planet of Ree.
It's somewhere off in a blue galaxy.
It's a long, long way away from here.
Don't try to walk, you're nowhere near.

It's a magical place with millions of trees
And twenty plus two fresh water seas.
It has two big moons up in the sky.
When you can't see one the other goes by.

There are lots of great critters that live in this place,
On the Planet of Ree in outer space.
They're all different sizes, some as small as a mouse.
There are sea beasties and dragons as big as a house.

The place is run by Wizards and Trees,
And a group of Sea Queens who care for the seas.
By themselves this work is too much for one,
But with many assistants they get it all done.

Ree wasn't always such a great place to stay.
A big disaster almost ate it away.
But all of its critters worked together, you see,
And solved Ree's big problem like a big family.

So have a good time as you go through this book.
At a brand new world you get to look.
You don't even have to leave your own room.
Just use imagination — take off and go ZOOM!

3

Big Trouble on Ree, Part One

Many thousands of years ago,
Exactly when I don't really know,
Ree was invaded by a horrible bunch
Of bug-looking Bugamites who loved to munch.

They munched plants and leaves of every kind
And tried to eat up all they could find.
But plants and trees make the air on Ree.
And without air-making plants, life couldn't be.

Where did these bugs come from? Again, I don't know.
But one thing was sure, they sure had to go.
Ree was in trouble, the worst trouble ever.
They needed a plan and it had to be clever.

In order to get Ree out of the soup
They'd have to work together like one giant group.
Or the place where they lived, the Planet of Ree,
Would soon be a part of history . . .

Before this time on the Planet of Ree
They didn't live like a big family.
All of its creatures just played in the sun
Looking out only for "Number One".

But they banded together, just like a team
And worked out the best plan you've ever seen.
They beat those Bugamites and that's for sure.
They came up with a sure-fire Bugamite cure.

How did they do it? How was it done?
At the end of this book you'll see how they won.
But before we go to the end of the book,
Here are some poems that give you a look
At the creatures that live on the Planet of Ree
Who weren't, but now are a big family.

We One Hundred Wizards

We are Wizards.
Did you know that?
We are magical people
From our shoes to our hat.

We're not very tall,
Maybe five feet two.
We have stars on our robes
And our robes are all blue.

And, we're pretty good
With the magic we use.
We could make a house float
Or whatever we choose.

Each Wizard has assistants.
We call them all "Erfs".
And without their help
Things would surely be worse.

There are one hundred Wizards
On the Planet of Ree.
We take care of the planet
With the help of the trees.

We're the wisest and the kindest
That you'll ever see,
We one hundred Wizards
From the Planet of Ree.

Erfs

These green people here are called the Erfs.
You can see by their looks they're not from Earth.
They're not very tall, only measure three feet.
Even though they're so small they sure like to eat!

They're honest and smart, tough and persistent
'Cause that's what it takes to be a Wizard's assistant.
They work very hard and have lots of fun.
I know you would like them if you ever met one.

This Erf is called "Jeeter" (Say "How do you do").
You'll hear more about him before this is through.
He sure looks cute and he's smarter than most.
He's not scared of anything, not even a ghost.

The Wizard and Jeeter work together just fine.
And Jeeter keeps the other assistants in line.
When they all go on journeys he's first out the door.
He's a curious Erf and he loves to explore.

The Erfs are important to the Wizards, you see.
They help them take care of the Planet of Ree.
There's a legend, they say, that's very well known
That Erfs become Wizards when they are full grown.

Sea Queens of Ree

While the Wizards take care of the land with the trees,
Who's taking care of Ree's blue seas?
Who takes care of Sea Beasties and fishes,
Makes sure that they're happy and grants all their wishes?

Who calms the storms when they get out of hand
And makes sure the storms don't ruin the land?
It's the Sea Queens who take care of all the seas
And are very good friends with Wizards and trees.

They ride on top Sea Beasties of gold
And have many great powers, so I've been told.
But who helps them out with this sea-watching chore?
They have Sea Princesses and that's what they're for!

There are 100 Sea Queens on the Planet of Ree
Because it takes that many to watch the seas
Sometimes at sunset on a sea to the East
You might see a Sea Queen on her mighty sea beast.

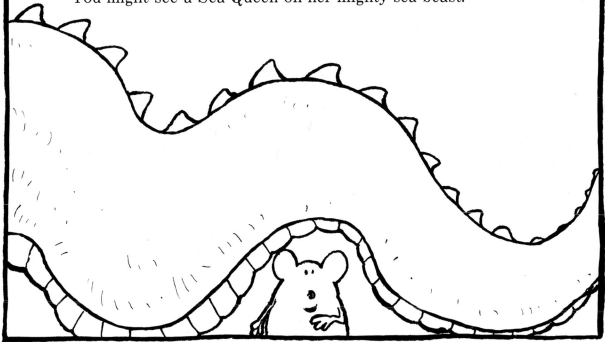

Sea Princesses

Sea Princesses help the Sea Queens get through
All of the sea work they have to do,
From watching the sea's beasties and colorful fishes
To sometimes even washing the dishes.

The Sea Princesses work hard all of the day
But they like it so much to them it's like play.
They're a little bit taller than the size of an Erf,
Like to ride sea beasties and swim in the surf.

They can breathe on the land and under the sea
And can talk to fishes like you talk to me.
Sea Princesses look cute but they're not fools
'Cause they learn many things in Sea Princess Schools.

Ree's Talking Trees

The talking trees of Planet Ree
Are really very strange.
When you get close to look at one
Then you'll see them change.

The talking trees of Planet Ree
Are not Earth trees, you see.
They have faces like people
And talk like you and me.

The talking trees of Planet Ree
Work with the Wizards closely,
Caring for that world of theirs
But soaking up sunshine mostly.

The talking trees of Planet Ree
Have helpers to help them out.
Small round things called "BeeBees"
Running errands all about.

The talking trees of Planet Ree
Are smart as smart can be.
And legends say when a Wizard grows old
He doesn't die, he becomes a tree.

BeeBees

These round little things are called BeeBees, you know.
A foot and a half is as high as they grow.

They can change their color whenever they please.
They're light and they're fast and can run at great speeds.

On the Planet of Ree all talking trees
Have hard working teams of helper BeeBees.

They live in the trees and keep them quite clean.
They're the best scouts and messengers a tree's ever seen.

At times they're mischievious but they're honest and true.
Without the round BeeBees, what would a tree do?

18

19

Sea Beasties, Sea Beasties

Sea Beasties, Sea Beasties
How big do you grow?
How deep can you swim?
Does anyone know?

Those colors on you,
So brilliant they gleam.
Those teeth in your mouth
More than I've ever seen.

You swim through the waters
Of the oceans of Ree
To places that I
Sure wish I could see.

Sea Beasties, Sea Beasties
Please take me along.
And as we swim onward
Sing a Sea Beasty song.

Gorbees Are Gorbees

These pink and purple porpoises
Swimming in the sea
Aren't pink and purple porpoises.
Not on the Planet Ree.

Those pink and purple porpoises
That swim and dive with ease
Aren't porpoises of any kind
But schools of friendly Gorbees.

Beware: Dragon

Here comes a big dragon through the green trees.
The ground rumbles whenever they walk.
Those dragons will do whatever they please.
They roar loudly whenever they talk.

They could crumble a boulder with a swish of their tail.
They can climb up huge mountains, no sweat.
But the one thing that makes a dragon turn pale
Is to get its four dragon feet wet.

They look mean on the outside, but they're not all that bad.
The Wizards, they keep them in line
Making sure that the dragons don't make anyone sad,
And posting "Beware: Dragon!" signs.

The Long-Legged Ploot

There's nothing as tall as a long-legged Ploot.
There's nothing as long as the Ploot's long snoot.
His feet are gigantic,
His smile so romantic,
You might even say that he's cute.

When he drinks up water he can drink a whole lake.
If you see a dry lake, it's a Ploot, no mistake.
He eats veggies too,
Much more than you do.
To him veggies are like chocolate cake.

He sails like a sailboat whenever he swims.
With his big round body and five fan-like fins
He sails 'cross the seas,
With the greatest of ease,
So don't try to race him 'cause the Ploot always wins.

A Floating Flying Finjerjin

A floating flying Finjerjin
Is something new to see.
He floats and flies across the sky
Gliding on the breeze.

A floating flying Finjerjin
Flies very well indeed.
He flies much better than a bird
And faster than a bee.

The floating flying Finjerjin
Has a trick, you see.
He's bigger than a frying pan
But lighter than a flea.

"Here" and "There"

These little things are called "Here" and "There".
Which way are they going? I couldn't say where.
When "Here" goes North, "There" wants to go South.
When "There" goes in, "Here" wants to go out.
One trouble these two will never find,
They'll never ever get hit from behind.

Splishes

There are so many Splishes in the seas of Ree
That if all of them swam past you and me
It would take us both two hundred years
To count each one of the Splishes' two ears.

They can out-smile anyone, this is quite true.
When you see a Splish smile you'll never be blue.
One thing is for sure, if you're in a jam
There's a million Splishes who will lend you a hand.

Snow Pookas, Snow Pookas,

Snow Pookas, Snow Pookas right over there.
They live up north in snow and cold air.

They look like white puffs with four legs and two arms,
But don't be afraid, they'll do you no harm.

They like to throw snowballs and slide on the ice.
They may be quite big, but they're really quite nice.

Snow Pookas have a call that they do
It sounds like this, Rahrooo! Rahrooo!

To find the Snow Pookas on the planet of Ree
Look for lots of cold snow, that's where they will be.

Flying Floojies

The flipping floating flying Floojies
Fly flapping through the trees.
The flipping floating flying Floojies
Fly fast all over Ree.

The flipping floating flying Floojies
Like flying best at night.
The flipping floating flying Floojies
Love the bright moonlight.

The flipping floating flying Floojies
Are like ping pong balls with wings.
Those flipping floating flying Floojies
Are funny flying things.

Funny Looking Islands?

If you walk by the ponds down by the sea
On this beautiful planet, the planet of Ree,
You'll see things bobbing in the water out there
Just floating around without a care.

"Those are funny looking islands!" you might say,
Until you see one of them swimming away.
Then you will see you made a mistake,
When this "funny looking island" climbs out of the lake!

You did not see an island or even a log.
What you saw in that pond was a very large frog!
Those "funny looking islands" near Ree's blue seas
Are not really islands, but giant froggies.

Spotted Tree Gings

What are those things
Way up in the trees?
I don't think they're birds
And they don't sound like bees.

They look sort of like lizards,
But they're certainly not.
They have long sticky tongues
That shoot out and go ZOT!

From branch to branch
They swing by their tails.
They travel through trees
Just like we do on trails!

So up in the trees
What are those things?
Well, that's a herd
Of spotted Tree Gings.

Big Trouble on Ree, Part Two

Now that you've seen what Ree's critters do
It's time that I finish telling you
How the big Bugamite battle was won,
Who did what and how it was done.

Just listen very closely and pay close attention
To how Bugamites were beaten by the Wizards' invention.
They formed a big team, as big as could be,
Of all of the critters that lived on Ree.

They worked out a plan. It took quite a few hours.
They found out that Bugamites loved Dandyboo flowers.
They'd lure the Bugamites to a place by the sea
Where the Wizards could ZAP them more easily.

They then made a trap, a giant cocoon,
Building all night long by the light of the moon.
When this was done, every critter on Ree
Picked every Dandyboo flower a critter could see.

The Wizards, the Erfs, the BeeBees, the Trees,
Sea Beasties, and Dragons and friendly Gorbees,
Finjerjins, Ploots, flying Floojies and fishes,
Sea Queens, their Princesses and even the Splishes
Brought Dandyboo flowers from wherever they grew
'Cross the land and the sea until they were through . . .

Then came the Bugamites under the powers
Of the sweet-smelling smell of the Dandyboo flowers.
They followed the smell into the cocoon
And were all locked inside by the late afternoon.

Then the one hundred Wizards of Planet Ree
Put their magic to work very carefully.
Even though the cocoon was a very large size,
When they waved all their hands, the cocoon it did rise.

It floated on up to a very high height.
Then the Wizards used magic with all of their might.
The cocoon exploded, it went KABLOOO!
Was that the end? No, the Wizards weren't through.

Zooming out of the cocoon and into the skies
Flew tons of Magic Butterflies.
Are the butterflies bad? Oh no, they're good.
They take care of the plants like a butterfly should.

From this point on in Ree's history
All the critters became a big family.
On the Planet of Ree, in good or bad weather,
These critters of Ree always stick together.

So that's what it's like
On the Planet of Ree!
It's a nice place to visit,
Don't you agree?

Are there anymore stories?
Do you want to hear more?
Well, watch for the next book
And see what's in store!

The Wizard Tells A Story Series:

Book #1 The Family of Ree™
ISBN 0-9617199-1-5
Book #2 Oh No! More Wizard Lessons!
ISBN 0-9617199-2-3

And Soon To Be Released:

Book #3 The Secret of Gorbee Grotto
ISBN 0-9617199-3-1

Book #0 The Family of Ree™
Children's Dictionary
ISBN 0-9617199-0-7

All correspondence and inquiries should be directed to:

Sutton Publications
14252 Culver Drive, Suite A-644
Irvine, Calif. 92714